SOREN THE SINGLE DAD

SUITOR'S CROSSING: THE CALDWELLS #3

HALLIE BENNETT

I0619497

Searching for more from Suitor's Crossing?

Check out the *Mountain Men of Suitor's Crossing* series here[1]!

---

1. https://www.amazon.com/dp/B0BZ3F9GG4

CHAPTER ONE

DIANA GOLDMAN

The house goes dark after the storm blows out the electricity. Strong winds batter the windows, shaking them in their old panes, and the rain blurs the forest of trees surrounding the cabin. Most people would take these as signs to batten down the hatches and remain safely within shelter.

Not me.

Call me crazy, but the lure of the storm is too great to resist, especially as a woman who has promised to stop curbing her desires, no matter how fraught with danger they may be. I want whimsy and magic. I want to romanticize my life like all those inspirational gurus say.

So, I grab my raincoat, tug on waterproof boots, and enter the storm. Icy drops sting my cheeks, but the slight pain energizes me. I feel like an ancient goddess gathering power from Mother Nature herself.

When I reach the cliffside of the mountain my rental cabin is perched on, I look down to see a river crashing against the rocks below. Trees bend and sway. Entranced, I stand there, letting the elements wash away the stress and worry I've felt lately, replacing them with a charged sense of rebirth. That's why I quit my old job and moved to Suitor's Crossing.

To break free from the constricting box I put myself in years ago.

To live a life worth living.

My eyes close and my head tips back in supplication, surrendering myself to an unknown—*but hopefully better*—future. Long minutes pass in this strange dichotomy of inner peace versus outer violence from the storm.

Eventually, the chill on my skin registers, and I decide it's time to head inside. But before I can move, two strong arms jerk me backward. My feet slip in the wet grass, causing us both to fall to the ground—or in my case, a large, warm body.

We roll over until an angry male face hovers above mine, his frustration palpable as he growls, "Are you out of your mind?"

I can't speak.

Confusion and wonder war within me at this stranger's appearance. Where did he come from? My closest neighbor is at least another mile down the road, and according to the Duncans, no one lives there while its owner travels abroad.

The mystery man continues his tirade. "What were you thinking, standing so close to the edge like that? Jumping into a raging river won't solve your problems. It'll only leave grief and heartbreak behind for your family and friends."

"Whoa, you've got it wrong. I wasn't going to jump." His wild assumption finally breaks through my frozen awe. My hands push at his shoulders—broad and sturdy as the boulders lining the trail to this spot on the mountain—and he cautiously shifts to the side, so he's not fully atop me anymore. I don't know why that causes a twinge of disappointment.

"Oh, really? Then what other reason could you possibly have for perching on the edge of a cliff during a fucking rainstorm?"

When he puts it like that, I realize how stupid it was coming out here. I got caught up in the storm's magic and let whimsical fantasies rule my actions rather than common sense. Now this stranger thinks I'm suicidal.

"I don't have a reasonable explanation for being out here," I admit. It's not like I'm going to share the personal transformation I'm undergoing with a stranger.

The rain increases in tempo, its icy sting battling the heat where our bodies are still pressed together. He's a freaking furnace. Hot, burly, and vibrating with annoyance, his giant body forms a cozy little cocoon around me. Well, as cozy as a girl can be pinned to the wet earth by a bearded mountain man during one of nature's tempests.

When he finally rolls completely off me, my chest expands on a long inhale that includes an enticing whiff of his spicy scent before being washed away by the rain. He offers a callused hand and hauls me to my feet with an ease that belies my considerable curves. I've always been short and stout—*yes, like the little teapot*—so his impressive show of strength puts all sorts of inconvenient thoughts in my head.

Like him hefting me into his muscular arms and whisking me away to his remote cabin in the woods, where he'll ravage my aching body and—

Holy hell, am I in desperate need of a man or what?

Is it possible to romanticize your life too much?

Shaking off the fantasy—because we've seen how well *those* are working for me tonight—I introduce myself with a trembling hand. "Diana Goldman. I'm staying at the Duncan cabin. Do you live around here?"

"Soren Caldwell." He jerks a thumb down the trail. "I'm your neighbor to the east. I didn't realize the Duncans had a guest; I was checking on the house before the storm worsened. Then I saw your shadowy figure up here." His roughened palm grazes mine for a brief second before dropping my hand like a hot potato.

"You're the sunflower mailbox!" My fingers snap in recognition. The black mailbox decorated with sunflower stickers brings a smile to my face every time I drive by it on my way home.

"Yeah... that's my daughter's favorite flower."

Daughter.

Shit, he's got a kid, which means he's probably married, and here I am imagining being fucked ten ways to Sunday by my would-be rescuer. *Not to mention keeping him from returning home to his family.* All because of my hare-brained scheme of pretending to be a freaking goddess of the storm.

Soren must think I'm a ridiculous ninny...

CHAPTER TWO

SOREN CALDWELL

With Sara Beth spending the weekend with her mom, I thought I'd catch up on household chores, maybe even grab a beer with one of my brothers at the Ole Aces. Then this storm kicked into high gear, and like a good neighbor, I figured I'd ensure the elderly Duncans' home was properly protected. Boarded-up windows. Electric fuses not left to spark if the power goes out.

I didn't expect to find a curvy beauty standing at the edge of the cliffside when I turned the corner of the cabin.

At first, I thought she was an apparition. No one lives out here now that the Duncans have moved closer to their grandchildren.

Then her head tipped up to the sky, illuminated by a lightning flash, and I knew she was real. And in danger.

"Come on. We've gotta get out of this storm before we catch pneumonia," I say, using a hand at her lower back to guide her away from the cliff's edge and toward the Duncan cabin.

"You don't have to walk me back." Diana quickens her steps, but she can't outpace my longer stride. "I'm sure your family is waiting anxiously for your safe return."

"My daughter is with her mother this weekend, so no one's waiting for me. I'm not letting you wander around the forest to find more trouble."

She huffs, swiping at the raindrops pelting her cheeks. "Trust me, I'm ready to bunk up for the night. The cabin is right there." Diana points to the rustic structure thirty feet ahead. "I can hardly miss my stop."

I ignore her protests. "Do you know how to light a fire? The Duncans don't own a generator, and with the power out, you're going to freeze without heat."

She reaches for the unlocked front door and steps inside the darkened living area with me glued to her heels. At this altitude, the cabin naturally maintains a cool interior. Perfect for summers, but not so great during the middle of a storm.

"There are plenty of blankets. I'll make do." A shiver wracks her body, but Diana tries to hide it by snagging the afghan folded over the couch and shaking it out.

"Nice try, but the sound of your teeth chattering threatens to drown out the rain." The obvious points of her nipples poke through her shirt, too. Her raincoat must have flapped open from the wind because it sure as shit didn't stop the wet t-shirt contest right in front of me. The soaked fabric clings to every inch of her curves in an obscene display—soft, sexy, and off-limits.

If I wanted sex this weekend, I would have accepted Beckett's invitation to hang out in Seattle. It's a bit of a drive from Suitor's Crossing, but worth the trip when it means avoiding messy attachments in our small town. Beckett already has a reputation with the women here, because my younger brother doesn't always think before he acts. *The bad boy of Suitor's Crossing.* At least that's what I've heard.

But I've got a daughter to protect.

I'm not going to jeopardize our quiet life by hooking up with a local woman and feeding the rumor mill.

Diana's not local, my mind whispers as I stoop to start a fire in the stone hearth. She's a temporary visitor. The Duncans list their house on those home-sharing sites, although they don't get a ton of takers due to the steep climb up the mountain.

Diana is clearly one of their guests.

Here today, gone tomorrow. Or Sunday.

Either way, she won't be a permanent fixture in town. No chance of us running into each other and making things awkward. Stoking the flames with a stab of the iron poker, I growl in frustration.

Am I seriously contemplating propositioning this woman?

"Easy, what did those logs ever do to you?" Diana's amused voice breaks through my musings. Her arms are crossed over her chest. Hiding her nipples but accentuating the heavy weights that would overflow my large palms.

Fuck. I toss the poker aside and stand, shifting on my feet to subtly adjust my growing erection. Seems even ice-cold jeans aren't enough to contain the motherfucker.

"You should change into dry clothes and then sit by the fire to warm up," I say, wondering where that leaves me. The smart thing to do would be to trek back down the gravel trail to my cabin, but strong winds and heavy rain will make the journey treacherous.

If a rogue branch hits me in the head, I could be knocked out and exposed to the elements for hours. My family wouldn't worry until a few days passed, since they know I tend to isolate, especially when Sara Beth is gone.

"The same can be said for you." Diana gestures to a door down the hall. "I've got a couple of men-sized things that might fit. Let me—"

"I don't want your boyfriend's shit," I grumble, my hackles immediately rising at the suggestion. Was this supposed to be a romantic vacation? Where is this asshole boyfriend? Diana's all alone up here, and anything could happen on the mountain.

Her brown eyes widen as she covers a cough of laughter. "Um, no... I don't have a boyfriend, and no, they don't belong to an ex either. Sometimes I just like having oversized clothing for comfort. Is that okay?"

The sass in her tone sends my dick punching forward in response, eager to tame her pretty little mouth, but I keep my cool. *Sort of.* I grunt my approval and turn to study the rest of the living room while she disappears into her bedroom.

This space is a wide open rectangle with the living area on one side and the kitchen on the other. One hallway splits the middle, leading to a bedroom and bathroom. It's a cozy set-up.

Too cozy.

There's nowhere to take refuge from Diana's enticing presence.

"Here you go." A long-sleeved tee and gray sweatpants land on the arm of the couch. "I'll give you a few minutes to change, then we can break out the alcohol to help warm up." She mutters something else under her breath, but I don't quite catch it before she's gone again.

Dragging my wet flannel off, I tug on the dry clothes and sigh as they cut into my body at different sections. I'm sure I look like the Hulk about to bust the seams on Diana's shirt and pants, but what other option do I have?

Besides, the uncomfortable dig of fabric into my shoulders and elbows is nothing compared to the thick ridge of arousal showcased down my thigh. The gray sweatshirt material molds to my cock like a vacuum-seal, which means hiding the monster length is damn near impossible.

My brothers would have a field day with this development. My sister, Kennedy, too. They think I need to relax. Have more fun. And a one-night stand with a stranger would be a hell of a lot of fun.

Until reality hits in the morning that I'm a single dad who's vowed to never let another woman hijack my life again.

CHAPTER THREE

DIANA

Shadows flicker across the ceiling as I tilt my head to down a second shot of tequila. My eyes squeeze shut with the burn of alcohol warming my throat and chest. It'll probably be my last for the night since I don't plan on getting drunk with a giant stranger sitting next to me.

A giant, *sexy* stranger.

Unbidden, my gaze drops to his lap where the largest dick imprint I've ever seen keeps a steady rush of arousal coursing through my body. I lick my lips. God, I *really* want to know what that feels like in my mouth. *In my pussy.*

It's been so long since I've felt anything but silicone between my thighs and breaking that celibate streak with the steel rod Soren's packing? A shiver of anticipation erupts at the possibility.

"Are you still cold? I can add another log to the fire." Soren shuffles toward the fireplace to toss a log on the crackling flames, causing the sweatpants to adhere to his firm ass.

Get a grip, Diana! I'm not usually an ass girl, but everything about this man has me aching in need. Suddenly, I'm a horny teenager instead of a respectable thirty-six-year-old woman.

"Thanks," I mumble, setting the empty glass tumbler on the floor beside me. We moved the coffee table out of the way, so the couch could be shoved closer to the fire. Now, we're both sitting on a faded rug with our backs leaning against the couch. "You said your daughter is with her mom this weekend. You're divorced?"

I'm desperate to know if he's single. If there's a shot for something more tonight.

If I'm brave enough to reach for it, that is.

"Never married. Got close, though." He scrubs a hand over his beard and sighs. "Marsha and I were high school sweethearts, then we had an on-again/off-again relationship until she got pregnant. I proposed, we set a date after Sara Beth's birth, then Marsha decided she wasn't ready to settle down and dumped both of us."

"I'm so sorry. That sounds horrible."

He shrugs, his broad shoulders stretching my old tee. "It was over a decade ago. We're on better terms now."

"But no chance of getting back together," I double-check for my own peace of mind. "And no one else has taken her spot yet."

"Nope, and no one will. Sara Beth is my life now. She's got plenty of family between my grandpa and siblings."

"How many? I've got a younger brother."

"Try having three younger brothers and a little sister. I'm the eldest." He finishes his tequila shot and rests his head on the sofa cushion.

"You mean the responsible, rule-following perfectionist? I know it well. My brother, Titus, is seven years younger than me—a surprise baby—and a whirlwind of rebellion. I love him, but his antics are hard on our parents."

"So, you make sure that whatever you do doesn't burden them, too," he finishes my unspoken words.

A tenuous bond of understanding twines between us.

Wrapping my arms around my bent knees, I lower my chin to the makeshift pillow. "That's part of the reason why you found me outside. Maybe I should have ignored my desire to join the storm. To absorb its chaotic power. But it seemed safe enough to enjoy a few minutes of freedom when I rarely give in to my more reckless cravings."

A rumble of curiosity comes from Soren. "What other reckless cravings do you have, Diana?"

There's no mistaking the note of lust in his voice, or the jerk of his cock and the tiniest of wet spots forming at the tip. He's leaking pre-cum? For *me*?

A flash of lightning brightens the windows surrounding us. The electricity I felt earlier on the cliffside has magnified—burns a fiery path through my veins, straight to my throbbing clit. Now is my chance to grab something for myself.

Stop curbing your desires.

Soren is a stranger, but he seems safe enough. He talked about his family. His daughter. A dangerous man doesn't discuss his personal life so casually, right?

"Diana?" His deep voice tickles my senses as amber eyes seek an answer to his question.

Swallowing my nerves, I unfold from the protective ball I formed and slowly move to straddle Soren's thick thighs, cautiously settling over his hard arousal before forcing my gaze up to meet his.

If I see rejection or disgust, I may melt into the floor, never to show my face around these parts again.

But it's not repulsion outlining his rugged features.

It's barely restrained desire.

This is happening—a passionate fling with my very own mountain man.

And I can't wait.

CHAPTER FOUR

SOREN

The cautious need in Diana's eyes is my undoing, along with the heat of her pussy bearing down on my dick. If this beautiful woman craves a night of reckless fucking, then count me in. I'm happy to oblige until dawn creeps over the horizon.

"Is this okay?" she asks hesitantly, biting her bottom lip.

"It's more than okay, firecracker." The endearment falls naturally. She's raw and sassy and sparking with pure energy. "But we might have a problem with protection. I don't have any. I haven't needed them in a long time."

Condoms haven't been on my radar for years.

"I'm on the pill, and my last health check-up was clear. We're good." Her hips roll over my lap, grinding her cunt on my aching dick.

"Um... more than good, baby." My hands creep under her shirt and tug it over her head to reveal flawless tits. "Damn," I mutter before diving forward to suck one of the cherry tips between my lips.

I alternate between each bud as Diana moans, riding my thigh like a world-class rodeo champ. "Clothes. Off. Now," I grunt, the caveman in me barely allowing for full sentences. She wriggles off me and divests herself of panties and leggings while I shuck off the clothes that barely fit anyway.

With my hard cock sticking straight up in the air, Diana bends down to suck on the mushroom head, her plump ass high in the air providing the perfect view.

"Goddamn, firecracker. This dirty little mouth is gonna make me cum." She moans and swallows deeper until the ridges of her throat rub along my cock. My fingers tangle in her hair. "Is that what you want? You want my cum filling this pretty mouth of yours?"

She hums in agreement, and that extra vibration pushes me over the edge as I come with a roar. Diana quickly swallows what she can, though my seed still overflows enough to drip down her chin.

It glistens under the firelight on her pale skin.

It's sexy as fuck and has me readying for a second round sooner than expected. I urge her off my dick in favor of lining her wet pussy up with my hardened cock and claim her reddened mouth with a possessive kiss.

"That was good, baby, but I need more than your talented mouth to satisfy me." My hand reaches beneath her to rub her clit. "I need your tight cunt milking my cock dry. You think you're up to it?"

She pants eagerly. "*Yes.*" Her cunt slams down, burying all ten inches of me in one fell swoop. We both cry out at the incredible sensation.

"You're so big," Diana breathes. She wiggles and whimpers on the thick impalement, and I grit my teeth at the strangling clasp of her pussy working my dick in rhythmic waves.

"The better to fuck you with," I tease, pinching a nipple between my thumb and forefinger.

Diana laughs breathlessly. Her fingers dig into my shoulders as she pulls me closer. "Then fuck me already, mountain man."

Growling, I shift us forward until she's flat on her back on the hardwood floor. The rug offers an inch-thick barrier, but not enough to provide real comfort. My arms slip under her knees, hefting her curvy body higher and changing the angle of where I'm hitting inside of her clenching channel.

"Oh... Oh... *Soren!*" She yelps, her head tilting back, exposing her neck to the firelight and drawing my attention to the heavy pulse. Bending my head, I suck on the sign of life, determined to leave my mark on her.

My heavy thrusts send her sliding across the floor until her hands reach up and brace against the stone lip of the hearth.

"Don't stop..." she begs.

"Don't worry, firecracker. You're gonna come for me once and then again, and then maybe I'll stuff this pussy full of my seed."

"Yes, please..." she pants.

Long, hard drives of my hips follow. It could be minutes or hours that we fuck in front of that fireplace. All I know is that Diana's pussy is the sweetest thing I've ever felt, and despite the tingling at the base of my spine—the need to fill her full of my cock and seed a primal obsession—I can't come yet.

I don't want to.

I can't.

I hold out until her body seizes up for the third time, her orgasm vibrating through her limbs, her voice hoarse from all of her screaming. Then I let go, sweat and calm binding us together as I collapse on top of her.

Fuck, that was intense.

And we've got the rest of the night to top it.

"DAD, SOMETHING'S WRONG with Whiskers."

I finish rinsing off my plate in the sink, then turn to Sara Beth, who's holding her white bunny close to her chest. "What do you mean?"

"He limps when he hops," she explains before setting him down and letting me witness the evidence for myself. His front paw twitches, and he begins limping before Sara Beth quickly scoops him up and feeds him a treat.

"Poor baby...." she coos to her fluffy charge. "He's hurt. We gotta take him to the vet."

Sighing, I check the time on my phone. We've got twenty minutes before Sara Beth needs to be in class, and there's no way Dr. Winston will be able to fit us in for an emergency appointment that soon. "Alright, I'll call the doctor and set up something for this afternoon. Go put him in his cage, then grab your backpack. We've got to jet."

Sara Beth looks like she's about to argue, but we don't compromise when it comes to school. There doesn't seem to be any other issue with Whiskers. He ate the treat just fine, so I'm guessing he'll be okay for a couple more hours before we can make it into the vet's office.

Once Sara Beth leaves the kitchen, I dial the veterinarian's number, and his secretary, Linda, picks up.

"Hey, Linda, this is Soren Caldwell. We have a limping bunny situation here, and I was hoping you could squeeze me into Dr. Winston's schedule today. After school, preferably." I know my daughter will want to be present when her prized bunny is examined.

"Oh, no, something's wrong with Whiskers?" The older woman loves all of her charges—dogs, cats, and bunnies included.

"Guess so. He started limping this morning. Looks to be his left front paw."

"We have an opening for 3:45. Is that okay?" Linda asks.

"Yep, that's fine."

"The new vet tech has been a lifesaver for us, allowing Dr. Winston to see more patients."

"Oh, that's nice," I say absentmindedly. The inner workings of the vet office don't matter much to me, but Linda is a talker, and if Dr. Winston hiring more help means my daughter's bunny gets seen sooner, all the better.

"I'm glad we were able to make something work."

"Yeah, me too," I say, missing the first part of Linda's monologue. "See you this afternoon."

A few minutes later, Sara Beth and I are on our way to the elementary school, but I can't help glancing in my rearview mirror as we drive down the mountain.

After our passionate night together, I snuck out on Diana the morning after, hoping to avoid an awkward conversation. Maybe that makes me an asshole, but I feared if I stayed any longer I might have asked her for the entire weekend together. Something that wouldn't have been smart.

She's long gone by now, I remind myself. *Probably.*

It's not like I've visited the cabin to check on her in the past three days, but the Duncans' guests rarely stayed past a weekend. Diana left Suitor's Crossing to return to her normal life. I'll never see her again.

For some reason, the realization makes my gut clench.

CHAPTER FIVE

DIANA

My phone dings with a notification from my Aunt Linda at the front desk. Dr. Winston's next appointment just checked in, which means I need to bring the pet and owner back to one of our sterilized exam rooms and do the initial intake.

Tossing the animal-safe disinfectant wipe I was using to clean up after our last patient, I hurry to the waiting room. This job is a godsend after the stress of burnout at my previous position in Everton. So many strays and wounded animals came through Dr. Marshall's veterinarian practice, yet the old miser refused to hire enough staff to adequately help patients.

I was one of the longest holdouts because I love animals so much. It gutted me to think about abandoning them, but Aunt Linda convinced me that any patient I saw would be better off if I took care of my health, too. No more double shifts or living off Taco Bell runs. So, when her boss started looking for a vet tech, she immediately suggested me, and after one interview, I was hired.

Dr. Winston is a way better boss than Dr. Marshall. Hotter, too. Not that I stare too much since he's hopelessly in love with his wife, and I've got the memory of a sexy mountain man keeping me occupied.

"Who's up, Aunt Linda?" I lean against the front counter as my eyes scan the room. A Chihuahua shivers in its owner's arms in the corner, while a cat's yowls emanate from a purple mesh carrier a few feet away.

My gaze skims over a large man in flannel and the little girl holding a bunny beside him before skittering to a halt and backtracking.

"Soren Caldwell, his daughter Sara Beth, and Whiskers, her bunny. Sara Beth, come on. It's your turn, honey." Aunt Linda's voice fades in and out as the family stands.

Oh my god. It's him. He's here.

With his daughter!

"Hi! I'm Diana." My wave is overly perky. So is my smile. Maybe that's why Soren is staring at me like I've grown two heads. *Or maybe he's freaking out as much as you are because he had his tongue and cock buried in your pussy mere days ago!* "Follow me, and we'll figure out what's going on with Whiskers."

"His paw is hurt," the girl says with a frown.

"Oh, no! Let's see if we can make him feel better, hmm?" A steady stream of bunny-centered conversation flows between us while I weigh Whiskers, consciously avoiding looking at Soren. It's not so easy to avoid the addictive scent of pine and spice that clings to him, though. The familiar smell sends a pleasurable shiver down my spine as I recall our night together.

Focus, Diana! You're a professional!

Dr. Winston knocks before entering the exam room minutes later, and I regret chatting with Sara Beth so much. With four of us—two men giant as fuck—the space becomes claustrophobic. I should have escaped already instead of lingering in the room to talk... and covertly ogle this little girl's dad.

"You said he's limping?"

Sara Beth nods while I add what I witnessed upon my initial exam. "He hopped fine a couple of times, then the limping started. No tenderness when I felt the injured leg."

"Thanks, Di," Dr. Winston says while conducting his own examination. "Let's get some X-rays to see what's going on."

I scoop Whiskers into my arms and exit the room quickly, bumping shoulders with Soren in one electric moment before scrambling down the hall.

CHAPTER SIX

SOREN

D iana is *here*. She works at the vet's office. Dr. Winston knows her well enough to call her *Di*. I choke back the inappropriate growl threatening to rumble out at that specific realization.

Does that mean she's staying at the Duncan cabin permanently?

Does she fucking *live* in Suitor's Crossing?

"I've got good news and bad news," Dr. Winston says, swiping across his tablet forty-five minutes later. He flips it over to show an X-ray of Whiskers's leg. "The good news is there's nothing wrong with this leg. It's perfectly healthy. The bad news is Whiskers was faking his injury for treats."

"What?" Disbelief straightens my spine. Now I've got a diabolical bunny on my hands along with the beautiful woman I never meant to see again. "He's faking it?"

"My guess is a sore paw earned him some extra love." Dr. Winston eyes Sara Beth in amusement. "Then, when it healed and the treats stopped, he figured he'd work the system to get them again."

"Bad bunny," Sara Beth scolds with an adorable scowl.

Bad fucking bunny.

This visit plus X-rays cost real money despite the fake injury, but it's not the money that concerns me. It's the surprise twist of finding Diana again, proving that my theory that she was long gone was wrong, and I don't know how to feel about the news.

If I'm honest, she hasn't been far from my mind this week. She's even infiltrated my dreams. But that's where her hold on me needs to end.

The whole reason I gave in to temptation was because I thought Diana would leave town. I wanted to keep things from getting messy. Guess the joke's on me because this already feels messy as fuck.

There's no way we can avoid each other when Sara Beth and I make regular visits to the vet for Whiskers.

What am I going to do?

CHAPTER SEVEN

DIANA

"Thanks for volunteering to help this weekend with the equine vaccinations. We don't normally deal with big animals, but Dr. Cabbage couldn't miss his daughter's college graduation, and they needed to get done."

"It's no problem," I say, standing next to Dr. Winston as he prepares our next patient for her vaccine. Frankly, I'm grateful for something to do.

While it's nice having weekends to myself, a luxury I haven't experienced in forever, this one's different. I want—no, *need*—to stay busy. To occupy my mind with something other than the last few days.

Because I had a one-night stand with my neighbor. A neighbor who frequents my workplace often thanks to his daughter's cute little bunny.

I'm still recovering from the shock of seeing Soren. So, an opportunity to redirect my thoughts from the growly mountain man who made me feel things I never felt before? Sign me up.

"What are these guys here for anyway?" I ask, petting the soft brown hair along the mare's muzzle. "I thought this was a resort, not a ranch."

"Hearthstone Lodge offers its clientele a wide range of activities during their stay. That includes horse tours on the local mountain trails."

"Oh, wow, that sounds fun. I've never ridden a horse before."

"You should sign up for one," he says.

"Don't I have to be a guest?"

"Nah, they open to the public a few weekends each month. Plus, I'm friends with the family who owns it, so you're good. You actually met one of the brothers: Soren Caldwell."

"Soren owns this place?" Good grief, I can't escape the man.

"Not him, specifically. It's been in his family for generations."

"So he works here."

"Most of their family works here. His brother, Ezra, is the one who manages it."

"I see." As if summoned by our conversation, the clip-clop of a horse nearing the stables sounds outside, and when I glance up, Soren sits astride a leather saddle in his usual uniform of jeans and flannel.

Whoa. Cowboy Mountain Man? Mountain Cowboy? Whatever he is, it is definitely working for me. But is that any surprise? Everything about him works for me.

If he were up for it, I wouldn't mind seeing him again outside of work and inside my bed.

But it's clear he only wanted a one-time thing, and judging by the shock on his face when he saw me again, he's far from open to rekindling our very brief relationship.

"Dr. Winston, what are you doing here?" Soren's gaze travels up and down my casual outfit. Jeans and a sweatshirt instead of scrubs.

"Dr. Cabbage had a graduation to attend today. I'm filling in with Diana's help."

Soren nods slowly, his gaze a sizzling beam across my body. "I forgot about Bethany's graduation." The gruff rumble of his voice reminds me of the dirty praise he whispered in my ear while buried deep inside my pussy, and my temperature increases a couple degrees. Sweat gathers uncomfortably beneath my hoodie. "I'll let you guys get to it. Don't mind me."

The next twenty minutes pass in a cloudy haze as I try not to ogle Soren, who's several stalls down from us. He's gentle while removing the riding elements from the horse. A low murmur tickles my senses as he talks to the large animal, and it soothes some of my nerves.

I already knew Soren was a good guy based on how he treated his daughter and Whiskers and shared about his family, but seeing more evidence of his kindness?

Ugh! My heart has zero chance to defend itself. Apparently, hot dads with a gentle streak for animals are my kryptonite.

When Dr. Winston finally packs his bag to signal we're done with the vaccinations, a whoosh of relief rushes from my lungs. I've got to get my head on straight, and it's not going to happen this close to my freaking dream guy.

We wave goodbye in the Hearthstone Lodge parking lot, and that should be my cue to leave.

So why do my feet follow the path right back to the stables? Because I'm a romantic sucker and weak for a certain grumpy mountain man.

Soren is brushing his horse, so I lean over the stall door and tentatively wave in greeting. "Can we talk?" I ask, fidgeting with a knot in the wood.

"Do you need something?" The only sign of his agitation is the flexing of his hand around the brush.

Be brave, Diana. A pathetically puny pep talk, but it's all I've got at the moment. "I feel like we should discuss what happened and how to move forward from here."

Soren sighs and pauses his rhythmic strokes along the horse's flank. He turns to face me. "Nothing's changed. We're strangers, and it's our own fault for not talking more before..." He waves his hand, alluding to our night together.

"Right. I just wanted you to know that I know what that was, and I don't want it to be awkward between us whenever you come in with Sara Beth and Whiskers."

His brow creases. "Okay."

"Okay. Have a good weekend." I force a smile and spin around to flee the premises. *So much for not being awkward.*

"Diana, wait," Soren calls out moments later. His boots slap across the concrete floor until he stops in front of me, a chastised expression on his rough-hewn features. "I owe you an apology. I'm sorry."

"For what?"

"For whatever that was back there, and for giving you the cold shoulder at the vet's office the other day. It threw me for a loop seeing you again. I figured you were a temporary guest at the Duncans' place, not a permanent resident. I don't..." He scrubs a hand down the back of his neck. "I try to avoid flings in town for Sara Beth's sake. I don't want gossip getting back to her."

"I would never—" I start.

"I know. I'm out of practice, and I guess it turns me into an asshole. It's been a long time since I've been with a woman, and if I'm being honest, if it was just sex, then maybe this would be easier. But I felt a connection that night; I like you. However inconvenient that may be."

Hope springs in my chest. "I like you, too," I admit. "Does that mean you want to see me again?"

"I shouldn't." That fledgling hope plummets in my stomach until he continues with a sheepish grin. "But, yeah, I would."

"I don't want to cause trouble in your life, especially with your daughter. We don't know what this is aside from that night being amazing." *Magical. A dream.* "Let's go on a first date and see where things go from there," I suggest. "Maybe we'll discover we have nothing in common, and we'll get this spark between us out of our systems."

"Don't say 'spark' too loud," he jokes.

"What do you mean?"

"You haven't heard about *heart sparks* yet?"

"You mean that soulmate thing?"

A bark of laughter erupts from his barrel chest, and the sight of his amusement— so different from his usual stoicism—brings a pleased blush to my cheeks. I did that. I brought on that happy flush to his tanned skin.

"That 'soulmate thing' is what Suitor's Crossing is built on. People meeting, the famous bridge, *heart sparks*."

Now that he mentions it, I do remember the huge sign welcoming people to town, hyping some legend of love. "You don't believe in it, though."

"Let's just say I thought I found mine early on and was sorely mistaken."

"Sara Beth's mom," I venture.

"Yeah."

"Does she still live in town?" If he wants to avoid gossip, going on a date with another woman while his baby mama lives nearby is a recipe for disaster.

"No, she lives in Seattle. She comes down every once in a while to see Sara Beth..." Soren trails off, then changes the subject. "So, that date. How about six o'clock tonight at Hatchet Crazy? I know it's a little early, but—"

"That's fine. I go to bed early anyway. I am not made for staying out late anymore. Not that I ever really did."

"Same. Responsible eldest child syndrome." We share a laugh of commiseration. "I'll pick you up from the Duncans'."

"Should we exchange numbers in case something happens?" I ask.

He agrees, and we switch our phones to input the numbers, then a minute later, I'm walking back to my car.

What an interesting turn of events.

Soren may doubt the credibility of *heart sparks*, and I can't say I've ever experienced love at first sight, or anything close to the feeling of a soulmate, but a seed of excitement burrows in my belly at the possibility.

Soulmate. *Heart sparks.*

Talk about romanticizing your life...

I got a new job in a new town, and a new love would be the perfect cherry on top.

CHAPTER EIGHT

SOREN

Axe-throwing for a first date may not be traditional, but I figured it might make conversation easier if we're focused on an activity. Hatchet Crazy opened seven months ago and has a lot of town buzz because of its mix of fun and food.

"This place is amazing." Diana looks around the rustic bar and grill in awe. It's not the fanciest place to take a woman, but I'm relieved that doesn't seem to matter to her. "Have you been here before?"

"My siblings and I will meet up every once in a while when we're feeling extra competitive. My brother Beckett is a beast with an axe, which shouldn't surprise me since he's a firefighter."

We take a seat at a wooden high-top table in front of an empty axe-throwing lane. For a Saturday night, it's not as packed as usual due to our early arrival, so we don't have to wait for one to become free.

"Really?" Diana glances up from the laminated menu in her hands. They serve basic burgers and fries with a few local specialty items, like Miss Patty's Rose Lemonades, which are usually only available in the fall at Apple Fest. "Do firemen require the use of axes a lot on the job?"

"According to Beckett, you'd be surprised," I drawl. Our family hears all sorts of crazy stories from him about the calls he gets on duty. "But enough about my brother. I want to learn about you."

Diana blushes and waits for our waitress to write down our drinks and food order before leaning forward. "There's not much to tell." She shrugs. "I've always loved animals, so vet med seemed like the natural path to take. I used to work at a super busy clinic in Everton. My boss pushed for long, strenuous hours, though. Which is why when my aunt suggested applying for the vet tech position here, I leapt at the opportunity."

I nod, grateful for her Aunt Linda's suggestion. If it weren't for her, we never would have met. "That's the job, but what about outside the nine to five?"

"Like, have I ever been married?" she asks with a raised brow. "The answer is no, and I've never gotten close either. I wasn't kidding about Dr. Marshall. I barely had time to relax on the couch and catch up on my favorite TV shows. My work-life balance was shit, so dating fell by the wayside."

"I get it," I say. "Dating hasn't been a priority for me either. Granted, my job is fairly flexible since I'm fortunate enough to work at our family's lodge, but Sara Beth's well-being has been my focus for the last decade."

"As it should be." Our food arrives—the Quadruple Slider Sampler for her, a buffalo burger for me—and Diana hums in delight at the tempting aromas wafting from the steaming baskets. "You're a good dad, and this looks damn delicious."

Our conversation continues in spurts as we dig into dinner, and I try to ignore the sounds of approval coming from across the table.

The uncomfortable bulge in my jeans proves how unsuccessful I am.

Damn... How can one woman make eating mini-cheeseburgers sound so sexy?

CHAPTER NINE

DIANA

"**R**eady to add a little danger to the evening?" Soren teases after we stack our empty food baskets at the center of the table. Dinner was delicious, though it was tough keeping up my side of the conversation when Soren's every move made my stomach flutter.

The bob of his Adam's apple while taking a drink. The flex of his forearm muscles when he opened the ketchup bottle for me. Small details that shouldn't mean anything have me practically panting in my seat.

"Danger? Has someone actually gotten injured here?" The restaurant made us sign a waiver upon entrance. I figured it was your basic legalese to cover their asses, but maybe they had a legitimate reason for the contracts.

"Not that I know of." Soren gently guides me away from our table and offers a small axe, worn handle facing me, once we are stationed in an open throwing lane. "The blades are dull as fuck. I could never chop wood with these."

An image of Soren shirtless, a plaid flannel tied around his thick waist, as he swings an axe down on a hefty log has my temperature rising. I'd pay good money to watch his muscles ripple and gleam with sweat.

So would a bunch of other women, I bet.

Raising the axe overhead with a flare of jealousy, I mimic the person a couple of lanes over from us and toss it toward the gouged wooden wall with a target painted on its center. The blade hits the wall, then bounces pathetically to the ground.

"Damn," I mutter under my breath. TV makes this look a lot simpler.

"Don't worry. Hardly anyone gets it right on the first try." Soren grabs the axe and hands it over again, but this time he adds instructions, standing behind me to direct my movements.

"Smooth move, mountain man."

"Just demonstrating proper technique, firecracker." His hot breath tickles my ear as he dips his head low. There's the barest brush of his lips on my neck before he steps back to give me room to throw.

I swing my arms forward—a brief worry of the handle accidentally slipping out of my sweaty grip and flying backwards to hit somebody in the head—before the axe flies through the air and lands with a thud on the outside of the target. It doesn't earn me any points if Soren and I were truly playing a game, but at least it stuck in the wood instead of rattling to the ground again.

It makes me feel strong to have embedded the blade in the wood, even those couple of inches.

"Good job," Soren praises. He pats my shoulder in approval, then yanks the blade out of the wall. "My turn."

This should be interesting... I cross my arms and watch avidly as Soren braces his feet shoulder-length apart to prepare for his throw. It's hot as hell, and I recall my earlier fantasy of him chopping wood.

"How often do you have to cut up firewood?"

"What?" he asks in surprise. The axe lands near the center of the target, of course.

"You said these blades literally won't make the cut for chopping wood. I'm just wondering how often you have to do that," I say nonchalantly. Like I'm not compiling a naughty cache of imaginary scenarios where my hardworking lumberjack neighbor steals me away to his remote cabin to ravage me until dawn.

"Well, I'm a mountain man like you so lovingly like to say," he teases, "So I have to do it quite often."

"Hmm... I'll have to visit one of those times."

"Or I can chop wood for you at the Duncans' place. Our stockpile at home is pretty high already."

"Even better." I grin in anticipation.

This first date is supposed to be a barometer test to see how well we get along. If there's something real here. If Soren is suggesting hanging out again—this time in a sexy woodchopping fantasy—then that must mean he wants more, right?

The rest of the evening flies by with us trading flirtatious taunts and tossing an axe at a wall until Soren drives me home. As we pass his cabin and the sunflower mailbox, I ask, "Where's Sara Beth tonight?"

"At my sister Kennedy's. Her husband is away for his job at McCoy Security, so she offered to have a sleepover at her place."

"Sounds fun! Who is Kennedy's husband? Someone from McCoy Security conducted a maintenance check on the security system at the clinic, so maybe I met him."

The man had been extremely attractive in a military-precision type of way with his short hair and neat appearance, and he'd definitely worn a gold wedding band on his finger.

"Wyatt, but you probably dealt with James or one of the other guys because Wyatt usually handles the physical bodyguard jobs. Like now, he's leading a team that's providing security for a three-day event in Seattle."

"Oh, wow." That must have been a boon for a small town security firm.

When Soren parks his truck in front of my cabin, we sit in silence for a beat before I ask a question that's been weighing on me all evening. "Does your daughter know you went on a date tonight?"

"Yes." He shifts to face me from the driver's seat, scrubs a hand over his beard, then shrugs. "I've never had to broach the topic of dating with her before, and I probably wouldn't have mentioned you yet, except she already met you at the veterinarian office. It seemed silly to keep you a secret after that."

"Understandable... How does she feel about you dating? She's not harboring any *Parent Trap* ideas about you and your ex, is she?"

"God, I hope not because that's never happening."

"*We are never, ever, ever...*" I sing instinctively, unable to let the opportunity pass.

Soren groans in mock annoyance with a hand to his heart. "Taylor Swift? Really?"

"Maybe, as a thirty-six-year-old woman, I should be embarrassed about listening to her, but she's only a year younger than me, so I'm not. We're basically peers," I joke.

"How do you know how old she is? I love Bon Iver, but I couldn't tell you his age."

"Her birthday is the day after mine, so it's one of the few celebrity facts I know because that kind of stuff is interesting to me."

A speculative look enters his eyes. "You know what? I do actually know Brad Pitt's birthday because it's the same day as mine. It was one of those 'On This Day' trivia facts."

"See? You get it."

"Guess I do." A half-grin shines from his handsome face, and I flush. Soren is too damn attractive for his own good. *For my own good.*

Struggling with the passenger door handle, I pop it open and hop down to the gravel drive with a huff. The cool mountain air is a welcome respite from the heat of the truck's cab, with Soren so close. His intoxicating scent. His giant, bear-like presence that makes me feel protected rather than intimidated.

"Whoa, where are you running off to so quickly?" Soren's fingers wrap around my arm and tug me to a stop outside the front door.

Facing him with a trembling smile, I avoid his gaze. "Nowhere. I just..." Words fail me. An overwhelming sense of rightness descends each time I'm around Soren. It grows stronger and stronger the longer I'm with him.

But that feeling also worries me.

This is our first official date. It went well, but the hopes I have far exceed the limits of a *getting-to-know-you* date. And I don't want to scare Soren off, especially when he was initially wary. With good cause—*his daughter.*

Soren studies my carefully arranged features. "What's wrong? What happened in the last five minutes to send you running from me?"

Damn the too-perceptive man.

"I'm not running from you per se," I stall, wondering how much I should reveal.

"Could have fooled me. One minute we're joking together, and the next you're fleeing my side like a bunny on the loose."

To be vulnerable or not.

That is the question.

"Come on, firecracker, don't hide now." He cups my cheek in his rough palm. "What happened to no longer curbing your desires, hmm? Shouldn't that apply to not keeping your thoughts a secret?"

"Just call me out, why don't you?" I mumble, glaring into his probing amber eyes.

Because he's right.

I'm supposed to be growing, not limiting myself. Romanticizing my life means hoping for the best, not escaping the potential of rejection before it can hurt me.

Allowing my head to bang against the front door, I grimace, then give in.

Becoming your best self can really suck sometimes.

"You... are... a dream come true, Soren. From the ridiculous conversation about celebrities to the way you care for Sara Beth. I've never met someone I've felt such an immediate connection to, and it got to be a little too much in the truck."

I don't think he expected that level of honesty because his body jerks, then tenses. *Oh god... He's about to race back down this mountain to escape the crazy lady who confessed her—*

"I feel the same way."

Wait, what?

"Do you know how much control it takes to not kiss you or grab your hand or toss you over my shoulder and take you home?" He dips his head to whisper his lips across mine. "A whole fucking ton. You're the first woman since Sara Beth's mom that I've wanted to pursue a serious relationship with, and what I felt for Marsha doesn't even come close to how I feel for you. But I want to do this right. We started fast; I don't want to burn out."

"Me neither."

"So, we do this the traditional way. We date and enjoy being together and I leave you with a kiss goodnight rather than tasting that sweet pussy of yours again," he growls, plunging his tongue into my mouth in a crude example of what he'd like to be doing instead.

My hands smooth up his chest to tangle in his hair, my fingernails digging into his scalp as we both groan in pleasure.

Slow.

I can work with that.

CHAPTER TEN

SOREN

"Heard you had a date. Who's the lucky woman?" Beckett asks after our family's weekly Sunday dinner together.

"Who spilled the beans? Sara Beth?" She's been peppering me with questions about last night ever since Kennedy dropped her off at home this morning.

"A buddy of mine saw you at Hatchet Crazy." Beckett drops onto the worn leather sofa in the living room and flips the TV on to a baseball game. He lowers the volume from the blasting eardrum level Gramps likes to keep it at, and we share a wry look.

We don't know how Griffen handles the noise. Our younger brother prefers peace and quiet. Something you'd think he'd get as our grandpa's live-in caretaker, but nope, Gramps is a social butterfly—always heading to the senior center and needing the TV and radio turned up to the highest settings.

Beckett's expression morphs into confusion a second later. "Wait, Sara Beth knows about her? It must be serious if you've already shared the dating news."

"Diana is the new vet tech at Dr. Winston's. When we brought Whiskers in for an injury he was faking, Sara Beth met her. It didn't seem worth hiding after that."

"Faking an injury?" I nod, and Beckett laughs before imitating Elmer Fudd. "That pesky wabbit!"

"Still watching cartoons?" Ezra, Beckett's more put-together twin, teases as he enters the room with his girl, Lauren, behind him and heads for a chair.

"As a matter of fact, yes, I am." Beckett proudly puffs his chest. "They're slower-paced and less visually stimulating, so they're relaxing to watch. Plus, there's the whole nostalgia aspect."

"He's got a point," Lauren agrees from her spot on Ezra's lap in the recliner. "I've read some articles discussing the potential benefits of older cartoons."

"For kids," Ezra jokes, pressing a kiss behind her ear.

Beckett rolls his eyes at his twin. "My TV watching habits aren't up for discussion. Soren's date on the other hand..."

I groan as they focus on me. At least the rest of the family is hanging out in the kitchen while finishing dessert, so I've only got three people to distract from this conversation before everyone dives into my personal life.

"You should invite her to the All Schools Day parade, so we can meet her."

"Bombard her with you hooligans? I don't think so."

"It'll happen eventually, and the parade will keep it low pressure. Lots of people around. Entertaining floats that make interrogations hard."

"Or I can just pop by the vet with Biscuit," Beckett threatens. He's the primary caretaker for the firehouse dog, which would make it entirely possible for him to ambush Diana at work.

"Fine, I'll ask Diana if she's free."

"Free for what?" My daughter walks into the room with Kennedy, Wyatt, Griffen, and Gramps not far behind. So much for avoiding the rest of my family poking their noses in my business.

"How would you feel about asking Diana to join us at the All Schools Day parade?"

Her face lights up. "That's a great idea. She can see me with my class!" The fourth graders are riding in a decorated trailer to celebrate the end of the school year. It's all Sara Beth's been talking about for the past month.

"Then it's settled." Kennedy claps her hands in finality. "Soren is bringing a date, and we all agree to be on our best behavior."

Beckett crosses his heart while sharing a mischievous smile with his twin.

Damn nosy siblings...

CHAPTER ELEVEN

DIANA

"That's Gramps's friend!" Sara Beth excitedly points at the street banner attached to a light pole. It has her great-grandpa's old pal's military portrait and his years of service listed. Based on what I've heard at the vet clinic this week, All Schools Day marks the end of the school year and the official start of summer activities, and I have to admit that the parade was super fun. Especially waving at Sara Beth as she and her classmates tossed candy to onlookers.

Apparently, Suitor's Crossing makes it a habit of celebrating a lot of holidays, which is why Main Street is decked out with Memorial Day banners, too. Pictures of local fallen soldiers hang on each light pole and will stay there for the rest of May.

"Buddy was a good man," Sara Beth's grandpa says, staring up at the vinyl banner waving in the breeze. "Gone too soon; may he rest in peace."

"Here's everyone's lemon shake-ups." Soren returns to our spot under the Blushing Brides Boutique awning. When he'd invited me to spend the day with his family, I'd been nervous.

Was it too soon?
Would they like me?

But the Caldwells immediately welcomed me into the fold and eased my fears by cracking jokes and teasing Soren about us. It's been a while since I've been part of such a tight-knit group. Most of my family, aside from Aunt Linda, lives across the country. I rarely saw them back when long work hours made it impossible to take time off, and now the distance is a big barrier.

"Mmm... What did you call these?" I ask, practically inhaling the ice-cold lemonade.

"A lemon shake-up," Sara Beth interjects before her dad can answer. "Because you shake it real hard to mix everything up." She demonstrates by aggressively jiggling the plastic tumbler in her hands. We laugh at her enthusiastic antics.

Soren's daughter is adorable. With dating so far removed from my thoughts back when I was too busy working at Dr. Marshall's, I rarely had time to consider how I'd feel dating a single dad. Children come with extra precautions, and at my age, most men have kids from previous relationships.

Maybe it helps that I've met Soren's ex during one of the weekend handoffs of Sara Beth, and there weren't any lingering feelings in the air between the co-parents.

Maybe it's just Soren.

Or Suitor's Crossing *heart sparks*.

But being a part of Sara Beth's life doesn't scare me. Soren and Marsha have a good system worked out. I'm just a bonus who gets to also enjoy the father-daughter duo.

"Are you doing okay? I know we can be a lot." Kennedy leans in close to check on me as we head toward the carnival set up across from the courthouse square.

"I'm good, thanks. You've all been super kind to the random stranger your brother brought as a tagalong."

Kennedy waves her hand in the air with a scoff. "You're hardly a stranger or a mere tagalong. You're important to Soren, or else he never would have considered asking you to join us. My older brother is extremely protective of our family." She takes a sip of her lemon shake-up. "I met your Aunt Linda at a bingo night with Gramps. She raved about you."

"Gotta love her enthusiasm." I blush, imagining the sorts of things my over-exuberant aunt might have shared.

"She's awesome and loves you very much. She's happy you're here and fancies herself a bit of a matchmaker now that you're dating Soren."

This I knew.

When Aunt Linda first heard about me and Soren—from a friend of a friend, because *small towns*—she'd called immediately to ask for all the details. The Caldwell family is Suitor's Crossing royalty, and to snag one of them romantically is akin to winning the lottery around these parts.

She couldn't wait to share the news about her *incredible niece* who landed Soren Caldwell in a flash of *heart sparks*.

Kennedy and I continue chatting while the guys buy tickets for games and rides. The rest of the day is a whirlwind with the countless number of people who stop to chat with the entire family. If I had any doubts about Aunt Linda's town royalty assessment, I know better now.

By the time Soren has me back in his cabin after dropping Sara Beth off at Kennedy's for another sleepover, I'm exhausted. "I had fun today. Your family is amazing." My hand lifts to cover a yawn.

"Thanks, they love you, too. I've never heard Griffen talk so much." Soren shakes his head in wonder as he shrugs off his jacket.

"What can I say? I bring out the best in people."

"You definitely bring the best out of me." He wraps his strong arms around me and drops a kiss on my forehead. Cuddling into his warmth, I hum in pleasure. Soren's protective embrace is my favorite place to be.

"Yeah?"

"Yeah."

"It must be this place," I murmur sleepily. "Suitor's Crossing has everything I didn't even know I was missing. It's more than having time to actually enjoy my life. It's the charming atmosphere, the kind people... and the hot mountain men." My chin tips upward as my brows waggle playfully.

"Happy to be of service, firecracker." Soren walks me back into my bedroom until we flop onto the bed. We agreed earlier that it's been a few weeks of dating and taking things slow, and we're both eager to spend a night in each other's arms again.

The slow burn is officially ending, *thank god*.

His lips cover my face in kisses before he pulls back, a twinkle in his eyes. "Although you forgot one major thing Suitor's Crossing has going for it."

"What?"

"*Heart sparks*."

CHAPTER TWELVE

SOREN

Diana beams at my addition to her list of town perks, then I pour every emotion I have into our kiss. *My heart spark.* Months ago, I didn't even believe in the town's legend of love. It was a myth. A sweet story to tell tourists.

But now I'm a believer.

Because of Diana.

Watching her with my daughter and the rest of my family solidified how good she is for me. She fits right in, and Sara Beth adores her. Even Marsha liked her upon their one and only meeting.

"*Heart spark*," Diana breathes, stretching her neck to give me more access to her body. I've been craving this alone time for weeks. Craving the freedom to taste every inch of her curves again. To feel the clasp of her tight pussy on my cock.

To claim her as my woman and more than the one-night stand we began as.

"Soren, I need you." She arches and writhes beneath me. Needy pants accompany her fumbling fingers as they try to unbutton my jeans.

"Don't worry, baby. I've got you." Rolling off the bed, I whip my clothes off and make quick work of Diana's, too, until we're both naked and vibrating with sexual tension.

My fingertips caress her full tits and round belly before landing on her inner thigh and gently pushing it wider. The smell of her arousal is a fucking aphrodisiac, and I can't help dropping to my knees and burying my face between her wet folds to inhale the delicious scent.

"Fuck, firecracker. It's been too long since I've had my tongue in this cunt."

Diana whimpers.

"That's what you need, isn't it? You need to cover my beard with these sticky sweet juices, so this tight pussy is ready to take my thick cock." The tip of my tongue burrows through her curls to find her clit and circle the engorged nub.

"Yes, Soren. *Please...*"

I'll never tire of hearing Diana's pleas for what only I can give her. I'm her man. It's my privilege to satisfy her every need, especially when that means multiple orgasms.

Teasing her clit with my tongue, I sink two fingers inside her channel to rub the extra sensitive ridges of her G-spot. The last time I got to touch Diana like this, we were strangers. I was determined to remain single. I didn't want a woman invading my life.

But my heart never stood a chance with Diana.

She's smart and sweet and gorgeous. She's a hard worker and kind. We laugh together over the silliest things, yet bond over our shared life experiences as the eldest of our siblings.

I can't get enough of her.

"Soren...!" The swift clamp of muscles around my fingers signals her climax as I work her through the waves wracking her soft body. I suck and lick until Diana shudders one last time, then I rise and position my throbbing cock at her entrance.

"Ready for more, baby?"

She nods, her throat undulating with a hard swallow. Gritting my teeth, I slowly stretch the tight ring of muscle with the wide head of my cock and sink deep, releasing a grunt of satisfaction when her curvy little body swallows my steel length whole.

"Such a pretty little cunt, baby. You take my dick so well. You were born for it. For me."

"Yes... Mmm... You're so big..." Diana mewls, wriggling under my heavy invasion. I brace myself on my elbows to lower my head and suck one of her nipples into my mouth. The flick of my tongue on the hard little berry increases the pressure of her pussy walls on my dick, strangling the thick intrusion.

Rocking forward, I grind my pelvis over her clit and release her nipple long enough to say, "I'm just right for you, firecracker."

And she's perfect for me.

Our bodies work together in tandem. *Give and take.* Diana guides my face up to meet her soft gaze, and we remain that way—connected on a soul-deep level as we each reach the pinnacle of pleasure.

This is only the beginning for us...

EPILOGUE

DIANA

D inner with the Caldwells is a riot.

Beckett's fireman stories. Griffen and Gramps's tales from the senior center. Ezra and Lauren's insight into the rich and famous. Then there's Kennedy and Wyatt, who are the calm oasis until Kennedy decides to wade in and one-up her brothers with a wry comment.

I freaking love it all.

They're my family now, including Soren and Sara Beth.

Oh, and I can't forget Whiskers! If it weren't for that troublemaking little bunny, who knows when Soren and I would have run into each other?

He hastened our journeys to each other with a little help from the magic of *heart sparks*.

"Aren't you happy you get to experience this kind of chaos every week?" Soren murmurs in my ear as his brothers start wrestling in the backyard after the dishes are done.

"Actually, I am. The Caldwells keep my life interesting." And one specific Caldwell keeps my life *magical, romantic*.

All the things I hoped for upon moving to Suitor's Crossing.

About the Author

Hallie prefers steamy, insta-love stories where the curvy girl finds love with a filthy-talking hero. And when she ran out of reading material, she decided to write her own stories. If you want a quick, hot read, she's your girl!

Read more at www.steamyromancereads.com.